we read to know we are not alone. —C. S. LEWIS

The book is here to stay. What we're doing is symbolic of the peaceful coexistence of the book and the computer. —VARTAN GREGORIAN

[A] book...unli...vision program, moving pictur... other "modern means of comm...n" ...can wait for years, yet be available at any moment when it happens to be needed. —Joseph Wood Krutch

To me, nothing can be more important than giving children books. —Fran Lebowitz, *The New York Times*, August, 1994

HEALING-PLACE OF THE SOUL
*Inscription on the library at the Ramesseum, Thebes, Egypt—Ramesses II*

WALT DISNEY There is more treasure in books than in all the pirates' loot on Treasure Island.

*Librarians: more powerful than a Google search, friendlier than a wiki, and the best natural language processor on the market.* —ERICA FIRMENT *Librarian Avenger*

A book is a friend; a good book is a good friend. It will talk to you when you want it to talk, and it will keep still when you want it to keep still; and there are not many friends who know enough to do that. —B. A. BILLINGSLY

Children are made readers in the laps of their parents. —Emilie Buchwald

The man who doesn't read good books has no advantage over the man who can't read them. —Mark Twain

# School Library Times

# LIBRARIAN RETIRES

Miss Lotty's first year at Sunrise, with Molly Brickmeyer, friend and dragon tamer.

### Time Has Come
### to Turn Page
### Says Miss Lotty

The beloved librarian checks herself out of Sunrise Elementary School Library this week. Students had hoped she would shelve plans for retirement, but Miss Lotty says her departure is long overdue. Happily, the librarian promises to remain in circulation and renew old friendships.

When asked to recall her fondest memory as a librarian, she replied, Dewey-eyed, "Twenty years ago, a little footnote of a girl named Molly Brickmeyer showed me how wrong I was to keep children from their books. I shed my scales, discarded my library dragon ways, and got in touch with my inner library goddess."

Miss Brickmeyer could not be reached for comment.

## FIRE SALE!

School Library upgrade requires the retirement of older assets. Available for immediate purchase are the following items in good working order:

- 16 mm film projector
- card catalog
- microfiche
- portable record player

For more information, call
555-SUNRISE

## ACKNOWLEDGMENTS

Special thanks to my wife, Traci, for all her encouragement on this project,
and to my sister, Nancy, who I can always count on to laugh at my jokes. Great thanks
also to Ted Graziano, the Barnes and Linder families, and to all my amazing nieces and
nephews, and to our good friends the Cook, Rich, and Wells families.

—*M. P. W.*

Published by
PEACHTREE PUBLISHERS
1700 Chattahoochee Avenue
Atlanta, Georgia 30318-2112
www.peachtree-online.com

Text © 2012 by Carmen Agra Deedy
Illustrations © 2012 by Michael P. White

Design and composition by Loraine M. Joyner

Illustrations are rendered in airbrush on 100% cotton archival watercolor paper;
title is hand lettered; text is typeset in Baskerville Infant.

Printed in April 2012 by Imago in Singapore
10 9 8 7 6 5 4 3 2 1
First Edition

**Library of Congress Cataloging-in-Publication Data**

Deedy, Carmen Agra.
  The return of the library dragon / written by Carmen Agra Deedy ; illustrated
by Michael P. White.
      p. cm.
  Summary: Miss Lotta Scales, a dragon also known as Miss Lotty the librarian,
wants to retire from taking care of the school's library but will not willingly stand
by and see her beloved books replaced by computers.
  ISBN 978-1-56145-621-5 / 1-56145-621-7
  [1. Librarians—Fiction. 2. Dragons—Fiction. 3. Libraries—Fiction. 4. Books—
Fiction. 5. Schools—Fiction.]  I. White, Michael P., ill. II. Title.
  PZ7.D3587Re 2012
  [E]—dc23
                              2011035265

# Return of the Library Dragon

CARMEN AGRA DEEDY

illustrated by

MICHAEL P. WHITE

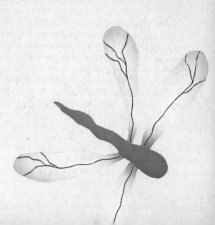

PEACHTREE
ATLANTA

For Ruby Bell Robison
—*C. A. D.*

For my daughter, Madeline Dorothy White.
Your presence in the world has changed everything
in my life in a most wonderful way.
—*M. P. W.*

Sunrise Elementary School had a BIG problem:
their beloved librarian, Miss Lotty, was…

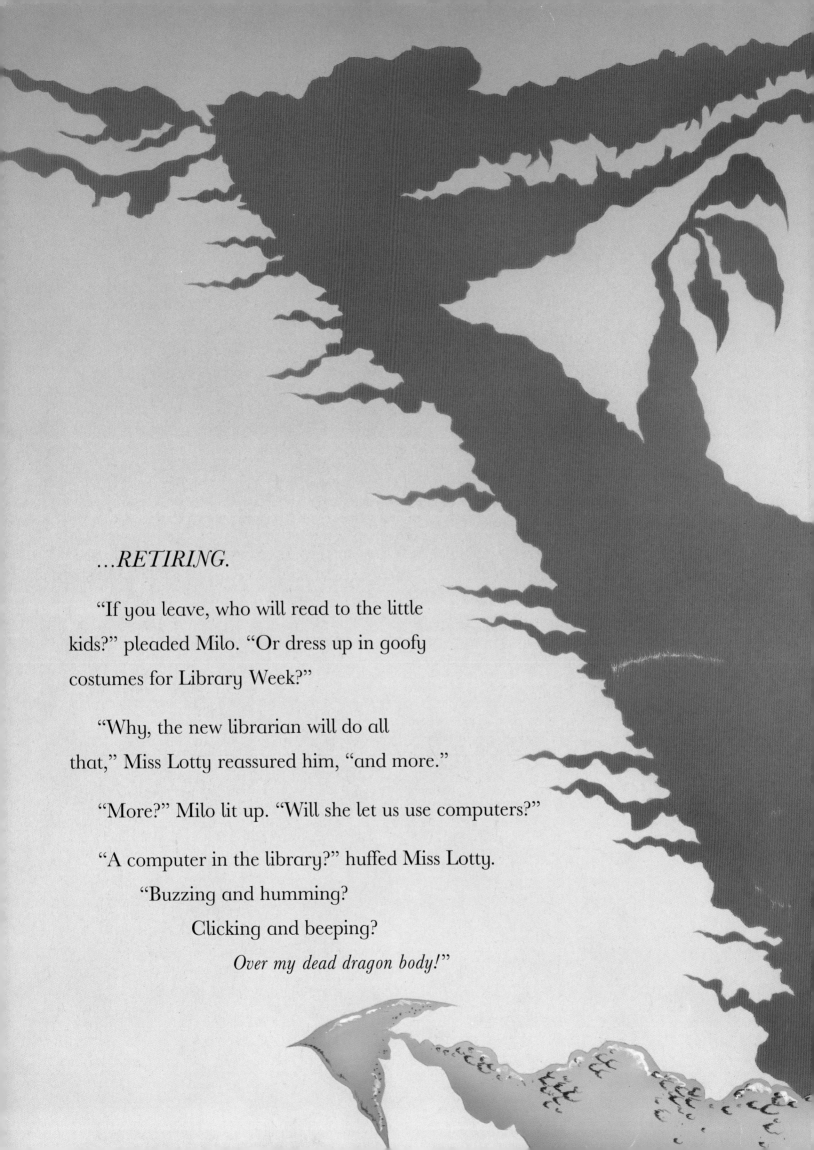

*...RETIRING.*

"If you leave, who will read to the little kids?" pleaded Milo. "Or dress up in goofy costumes for Library Week?"

"Why, the new librarian will do all that," Miss Lotty reassured him, "and more."

"More?" Milo lit up. "Will she let us use computers?"

"A computer in the library?" huffed Miss Lotty.
 "Buzzing and humming?
  Clicking and beeping?
   *Over my dead dragon body!*"

Milo blinked. For an instant, his sweet librarian had appeared quite dragon-like.

But Miss Lotty didn't feel dragonish for long.
Retirement was one blissful day away!

That night she fell into a peaceful slumber, counting children's books
instead of sheep. Of course, she knew nothing of the delivery truck
heading toward the library. It was loaded with trouble. BIG TROUBLE.

The following morning, Miss Lotty found a very unhappy Milo waiting for her.

"They're all g-g-gone!" he stammered.

"Gone?" she asked.

"The BOOKS are gone!"

Miss Lotty's tail gave a dangerous twitch.

"Who would dare take our books?"

"Central Office," gulped Milo. "And they sent a guy who says he's IT."

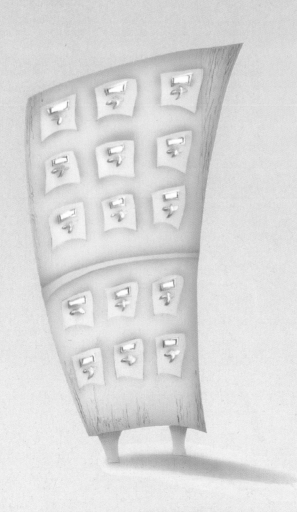

The library doors swung open.

"Come on in!" boomed a wiry little man. "The name's Krochip. Mike Krochip."

"Did he say microchip?" asked Milo.

Miss Lotty didn't answer. Her eyes scanned the empty shelves. "What have you done with our books?" A wisp of pale smoke escaped her lips. "You do know this is a library?"

"It's better than a library," chirped Mike Krochip.
"It's Media World! The new Sunrise Cybrary!"

"No…books?" Miss Lotty felt herself growing oddly warm.

"It's a brave new world." Krochip beamed at Lotty. "Books stain and tear and take up room. Check out the Book-Be-Gone 5000. It'll kindle your fire!"

"Pardon me, mister." It was Milo. Other children had gathered behind him to protest the library booknapping. "We'd like our books back, um, please."

Mike Krochip's brain short-circuited. "You want them back? But why, when you could have 10,000 books in one handy little—"

"Because," said Milo, "10,000 books on a screen all look the same."

And a third-grader added…

"Right, but 10,000 books in a library all look and feel different."

"And all I need to upload a book is my brain."

"My grandma can read me the very same book her grandma read to her."

THE MOLAR EXPRESS

Stinkerella

James and the Giant Leech

NEGA STRONA

SNUFF THE MAGIC DRAGON

Furious George

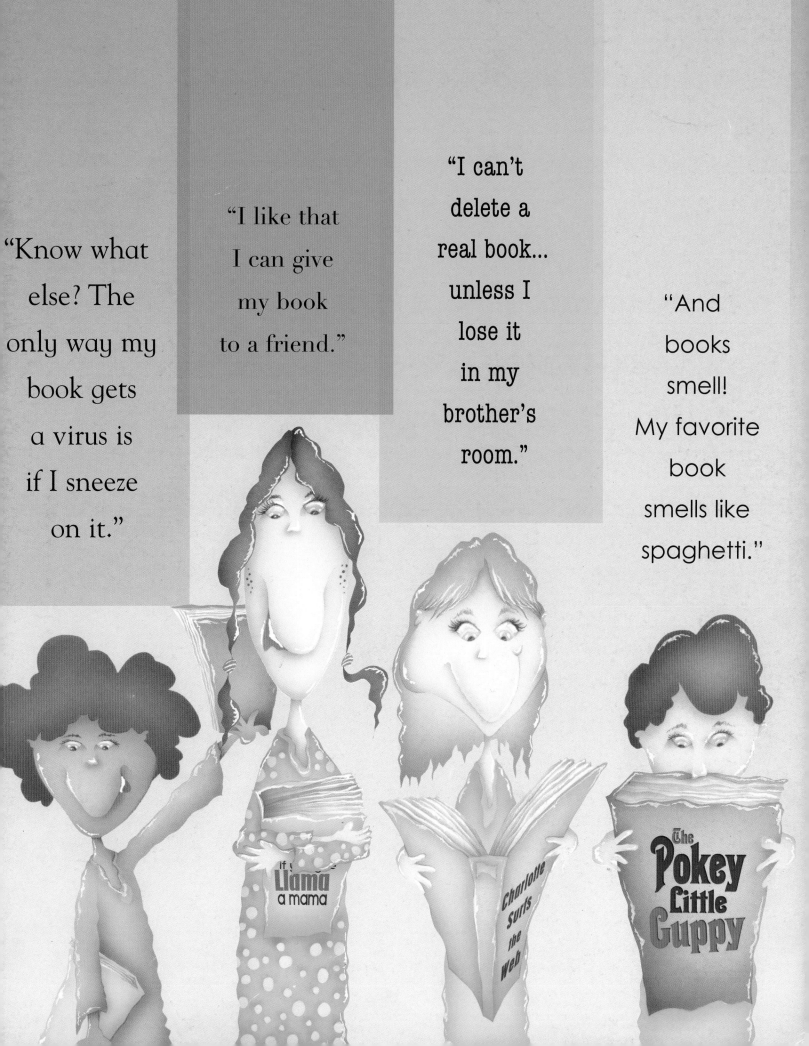

"Know what else? The only way my book gets a virus is if I sneeze on it."

"I like that I can give my book to a friend."

"I can't delete a real book... unless I lose it in my brother's room."

"And books smell! My favorite book smells like spaghetti."

"If you've never really loved a book," said Milo, "maybe nobody can explain it to you."

Krochip frowned.

Lotty looked smug.

And a fourth-grader turned on a MePod. "This is AWESOME!" she squealed.

The other children crowded around.

Even Milo.

Now it was Krochip's turn to gloat.

"Ha! Give me a month. These kids won't remember what a book looks like!" He loosened his tie. "Golly, is it hot in here, Miss Lotty?"

"That's Lotta Scales to you, little mister!"

And the Library Dragon...

# ...RETURNED!

"You bring back every last library book or I'll melt your motherboard !" roared Lotta Scales.

Mike Krochip and the stampeding children almost knocked over a young woman in the hallway.

"I wouldn't go in there if I were you!" he cried. "That librarian's a REAL dragon!"

"Oh, my." The sweet young redhead bit her lip. "Not again."

Meanwhile, Lotta Scales, the bad girl of the book world, wrestled the Cyberbeast. "No books?" rumbled the dragon. "Why, I'll eat every last byte before I let them take my library!"

Milo watched in awe. It's not every day you see your librarian eat a laptop.

…and a white board.

…and eight printers.

…and sixty-five tablets.

"Stop already!" he cried. "You're going to have a six-week bellyache!"

Miss Lotta Scales snatched Milo off the ground and eyed him with curiosity. "Do I know you, small mammal?" she grunted.

"Sure you do. I'm your best reader," said Milo. "Come on, Miss Lotty, I know you're still in there!"

They were interrupted by a knock
on the door. "Great balls of fire!"
crackled the dragon. "What now?"

"May I come in?"

"It's me, Molly. Molly Brickmeyer."

*"Molly?"* Lotta Scales took a trembling step toward the girl who'd once helped her shed her scales.

The dragon groaned.

"What's wrong?" Molly asked.

"They took our books!"

"Don't worry," said Molly, "The books will be back tomorrow. I told the principal I couldn't possibly take the job if—"

"Take the job?" Lotta Scales looked at Molly in wonder. "You're the new librarian?"

"I was going to surprise you," said Molly. She patted the giant beast's snout and whispered, "I learned from the best, you know."

And for only the second time in her life,
the Library Dragon's scales began to fall with a

clickety-clack,

clickety-clack…

...clickety-clack.

Miss Lotty was back.

"Just look at this mess," muttered Molly. "I love technology too. But our kids need a library where they can UNPLUG, for the love of books."

Molly's ears began to grow warm. "A children's cybrary at Sunrise? *Over my dead dragon body!*"

Miss Lotty sighed. The library was safe again, for now. She could pass the torch.

"Milo, meet your new"—she hesitated—"media-library-cyber-book specialist."

"Thank you," said Molly with a grin, "but I prefer…

Once you learn to read, you will be forever free. —FREDERICK DOUGLASS

So please, oh, PLEASE, we beg, we pray, Go throw your TV set away, And in its place you can install, A lovely bookshelf on the wall. —ROALD DAHL

The love of learning, the sequestered nooks, and all the sweet serenity of books. —HENRY WADSWORTH LONGFELLOW

Books are not made for furniture, but there is nothing else that so beautifully furnishes a house. —Henry Ward Beecher

I CANNOT LIVE WITHOUT BOOKS. —Thomas Jefferson

When I get a little money, I buy books; and if there is any left, I buy food and clothes. —ERASMUS

You don't have to burn books to destroy a culture. Just get people to stop reading them. —RAY BRADBURY

Never judge a book by its movie. —J.W. Eagan

A book is the most effective weapon against intolerance and ignorance. —LYNDON BAINES JOHNSON

LIBRARIANS ARE FROM VENUS; TECHNOLOGISTS ARE FROM MARS. —Doug Johnson

Oh, magic hour, when a child first knows she can read printed words. —Betty Smith, A TREE GROWS IN BROOKLYN

My library was dukedom large enough. —William Shakespeare

There is no frigate like a book to take us lands away...